Foreword

Who would have known that cleaning out one of the cupboards in my mother's house would lead to a story about a Viking, a dragon and a volcano. But it did.

It helped that by coincidence, there was a volcano erupting at the same time in Iceland, the status of which was meticulously updated on a daily basis by my good friend, author and illustrator, Michelle Gaskell.

Teaching poetry at both primary and secondary grades, I have come to realise how our education systems work to decimate any love of poetry that children hold. My desire is to change that.

So this tale of valour, Vikings, volcanos and vafrous dragons is a rhyme.

Poetry is music, it stimulates the same part of the brain as music: the right hemisphere; and at the same time it stimulates imagination, vocabulary and creative thinking. How cool is that for children and adults alike?

Out of a poem, a waterfall of magic pours; it creates an enchanting world where rhythm, rhyme and tone encourage laughter, reading, writing and speaking. What could be more fantastic than that?

All children should have the chance to love poetry, to learn at least one poem that they will cherish forever, and to be able to recite it with fond memories.

Who knows, one day Erik and the Volcano might just be one of them.

Erik and the Volcano

Sarah Froggatt

This is a work of fiction. All names, characters, places and incidents either are the product of the author's imagination or are used fictitiously, and any resemblance to any actual persons, living or dead, events, or locales is entirely coincidental.

© Erik and the Volcano 2018
Text copyright © Sarah Froggatt 2018
Cover images copyright © Sarah Froggatt 2018
© BrooksBooks.co 2018

First published in Singapore and UK on 20th November 2014
BrooksBooksCo in association with DiscoverEnglish
and CreateSpace

All rights reserved. No part of this book may be reproduced or transmitted in any form or by any means, electronic or mechanical, including photocopying, recording, or by any information storage and retrieval system, without permission in writing from the copyright owner.

ISBN 13: Soft Cover 978-1501074059
ISBN 10: 1501074059

The right of Sarah Froggatt to be identified as the author of this work has been asserted by her in accordance with the Copyright, Design and Patents Act 1988.

www.BrooksBooks.co
www.DiscoverEnglish.Education

Erik and the Volcano

There wasn't much to do or say
until that fateful autumn day.

Erik had an itchy hunch,
So he gobbled up his lunch.
That rumbling in his tummy,
Was really not so funny.

The ground began to twist and shake,
And Erik's knees began to quake!
Whatever could it be?
He'd have to go and see.

He had to catch the beast,
That rumbled in the east.
So he wore his woolly vest,
And set out upon his quest.

He walked a week or more,
Towards that beastly roar.
But he hadn't got a clue,
Of really what to do.

At first the drgaon shook his head,
'I'm much too tired,' he wheezed and said.
'I've puffed out fire all day,
I'm rather tired of play.'

'But I must defeat the beast
That rumbles in the east!'
Erik stamped his foot down hard.
'And I need a bodyguard!'

From where they saw the beast,
That rumbled in the east.

With puffs of smoke from out its nose,
That made them sneeze and curl their toes.

The volcano gave a little snort,
And cleared her throat in retort,
'I'll have you know, it's not a nose,
Although it often blows.
A caldera is its name,
It's what gives me all the fame.'

'I planned my spectacle to show
My brightest pyroclastic flow.
I cannot entertain requests
From Vikings dressed in woolly vests.'

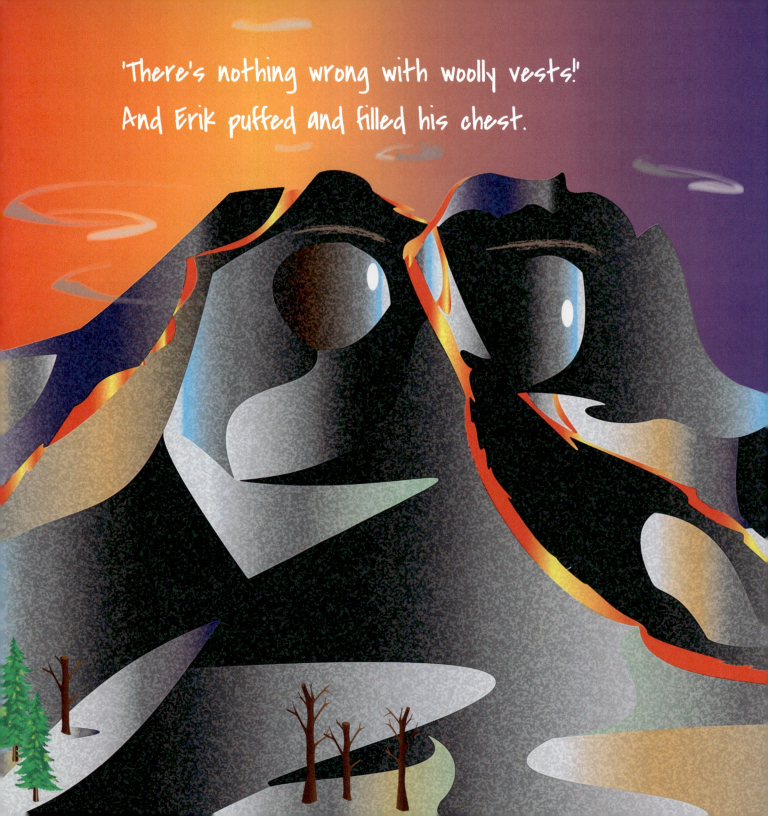

Bert bowed before the rumbling beast,
Whose spitting he'd just ceased.
He waived his tail and coughed some smoke,
Chuffed at his super masterstroke.

And Bert, I promise I'll be good,
And not destroy the neighbourhood
With dust and fire and lava too,
As grand volcanos never do.'

And all the world said, 'Erik's best,
This Viking in his woolly vest!'

About the Author

Storytelling and writing have been my passion since young. My father told me stories about two naughty monkeys named Hoko and Poko who lived amongst the banana trees in Jamaica, when I could not sleep at night.

His mother had told him the same tales.

When my boys were younger, I too created adventures for my own two cheeky monkeys. Encouraging my boys to join in; sometimes we would end up on a wild chase across Antarctica or falling into some mysterious land.

As a child, I loved illustrated stories: often disappointed whenever I picked up a book that did not have a picture or an image. I am still mesmerised when I read the fairy tales illustrated by Edmund Dulac or The Arabian Nights and even Quentin Blake's illustrations of Roald Dahl stories.

I hand illustrate my books - they are an extension of the words and ideas in my head.

I could never imagine a world without books and stories and hope that children everywhere will continue to read and love books for all eternity.

Animal Tails	Mayan Cocoa
The Balloon Ride	
Leopard Spots	Rotten Eggs
Rhino Itch	
Orangutan Swing	My Curious Brain of Noise
Artful Art & Friends	

Printed in Great Britain
by Amazon